# Birthday TREASURE

Are you ready for a story, Poppy Cat . . . ?

It was Poppy Cat's **birthday** and her friends were gathered in the **garden** with a **delicious** surprise!

"Happy birthday, Poppy Cat!"

NEXT were **lots** of exciting presents!

A **pretty** pink hat

from Alma...

a **pair** of binoculars

from Zuzu...

a **trumpet**

from Mo...

a **giant** pop-up inflatable raft

from Owl...

and a **plastic cow**

from Egbert!

It was a **treasure map** leading to the **Mystery Jungle!** But who was it from?

"**Come on,** let's go!" said Poppy Cat.

Soon the friends were on their way, rising high into the sky.

In no time they were hovering over the **Mystery Jungle**. They were about to **land** when they **spotted** their friend Egbert.

"**HELLO** Egbert!"

"I'm **NOT** Egbert!" he cried.

"I'm **Carlito** the **Itchy Mosquito!**"

And he started . . .

buzz

buzz

buzzing

all around the **balloon!**

"Watch out, Egbert!" they all cried,

but **oh no!** Carlito the Itchy Mosquito **pricked** a **big** hole in the balloon . . .

and then **buzzed** off!

**Down,**

**down,**

**down**

sailed the hot air balloon
till it landed, **PLOP!**

"Don't worry everyone, I've got JUST the **thing** to **rescue** us!" called Poppy Cat.

She **pulled** out the . . .

**giant inflatable raft**

and the **treasure** **map**...

and they all **floated** **safely** to shore.

On the **other** side, Poppy Cat saw **ALL** of her **friends!**

Surprise!

They had **come** to wish Poppy Cat a **very** happy **birthday!**

"Yes!" giggled Zuzu, Owl, Mo and Alma.
"No wonder my **presents** were so useful!" laughed Poppy Cat.

Poppy Cat and her friends had a **wonderful party** in the **Mystery Jungle**. They **danced** and **played** games and ate cake ALL day.

When they arrived home Poppy Cat thanked her friends, and they all promised to go on another adventure VERY soon.

"Thank you!"

"See you soon!"